Spring is Here

Taro Gomi

A TRUMPET CLUB SPECIAL EDITION

Spring is here.

The snow melts.

The earth is fresh.

The grass sprouts.

The flowers bloom.

The grass grows.

The winds blow.

The storms rage.

The quiet harvest arrives.

The snow falls.

The children play.

The world is hushed.

The world is white.

The snow melts.

The calf has grown.

Spring is here.